OUTLAWS PUBLISHING

THE DARK SKIES OVER AUTUMN

LOUISE RIVEIRO – MITCHELL

For information contact: info@outlawspublishing.com
Cover design by Outlaws Publishing
Published by Outlaws Publishing
May 2024
10987654321

Dedication

I will like to dedicate this book two individuals who are no longer with us but who are greatly missed.

Paul M. Fiore. A man who's smile could light up a room with his humor and could turn even the darkest days into sunshine. Your positive attitude and compassion for our students was a breath of fresh air. You gave them the courage to reach for the stars and beyond. You not only walked into the lives of those 14 students that year, you also won their hearts. Taken from us on that tragic day, Sept 11, we will always remember you as that special soul that honored them with your presence and changed their hearts and souls forever. Teacher and friend, you lit a glow in all of your students that will shine forever and a part of you will live on in those 14 students.

John W. Wilson who was the inspiration for both Chance McCord and Trace Cooper. Your encouragement and faith in my work was always there. The Cherokee cowboy was never too busy to offer a word of help for "Autumn" My one regret is you will not see this book, but I know if there is a way you already have. They called you home too soon my friend, such a pity we can't change what was meant to be. But I have been honored to know no braver man than Mtncherokee

August 1935 – June 2003

Rest peacefully my friend

To the Native Americans may the words on these pages from this humble person bring honor to all of you as many of you have honored me with your friendship. Wakan Tanka niya waste pelo (May the Great Holy Mystery Spirit bless you)

Chapter 1

On that bright sunny morning July 4, 1876, Colorado Springs like many other towns around the country were preparing for a day of celebration. Everybody was excited about the holiday and with the talk of Colorado becoming a state this year would be a special celebration.

As the morning sunlight streamed into the upstairs bedroom window it dances across Shayleen Cooper's face waking her up. She gazes to her side and smiles at the man sleeping beside her. Though three years had passed, she loves this mountain man as much, if not more than the day she said those vows. She slowly moves so as not to disturb him and gets out of bed and walks over to the window.

All that has happened that day since she came back from back east. Colorado Springs was growing by leaps and bounds and there was talk that the territory would soon become a state, it seemed that that world Shayleen grew up in was forever gone. But she still had Trace. Their marriage was a new beginning of a new life for her. She had settled down and was now the wife of a rancher. No longer that tomboy who would ride across the country like some wild mustang. She turns and smiles as she counts her blessings. Looking over to the far side of the room, sleeping in their cradles were the golden haired six-month old twins, Colleen and Katherine. She smiled as she remembers the first time she saw Trace, sitting in the rocking chair holding both of his 'little ladies' as he called them.

Mountain man Trace Cooper was content to be with his little ladies. Across the hall and still asleep was Michael Thomas, his fiery red hair earned him the nickname of Mick from his grandfather. It was Tom, Chance, Buck and yes, even Trace who decided the boy should have a horse, after all he did live on a ranch. It was Buck and Chance who managed to find the perfect little pony and just perfect for Mick. It was the daily ritual to get Mick out of the house and on the pony before his mom knew what had happened. It was then that they had him ride up to the kitchen window and wave to her. It was Buck who would take him for hours to the range and teach him to understand, not just the animals, but nature also.

Shayleen smiles as she thinks of her father, these children have given him a new life in his golden years. It's true Shayleen was the apple of his eye and he loved her dearly, but these three little ones were the blessing he had prayed for all these years. Life had been good to Shayleen also, she had Trace and three beautiful children and together with Tom, they had one of the finest ranches in the territory. Trace's wandering days were over, he had found a real home and his heart song. Shayleen turned as she heard her name. "Autumn." She turns from the window and walks slowly toward the bed. She climbs back in bed and nestles close to him. "You know have to get started …."

He smiles at her, "it's just what I was thinking," He draws her closer to him.

She gently pushes him back, "I meant we have to get started for town. I promised Charity and Chance we'd help with …"

He gently kisses her lips, "we will after we finish here." With that he kisses her again and she places her arms around his neck. He smiles at her, "what about Chance and Charity?" He looks at her, "they can find their own bed." He loved this woman with his whole heart and soul.

She smiles up at him, "Trace Cooper, are you trying to seduce me? You do realize I am a married woman."

"Oh I realize that Ma'am and I know that the man lucky enough to be married to you is the luckiest man on this earth."

Back in town, Chance smiles down at his wife as she's watching him trying to center the sign for the July Fourth celebration. He and the reverend have been trying for the better part of two hours under Charity's direction trying to center the banner.

"Charity, is it right now?"

Mrs. McCord looks up and smiles at her husband as their three-month daughter squirms in her arms," no, seems to need a little more to the right dear." Chance looks at his father-in-law and shakes his head, "you do know we had it that way four times already."

The older man smiles at him, "a word of advice Son?"

Chance looks at him, "Sir?"

"Just agree with her, it always works."

Chance nods and moves the banner once again, then looks at his wife. A smile comes to her face, "that's perfect. Okay hang it." Chance looks at his father-in-law who smiles. "Works every time Son."

Charity looks up at her husband, she had to admit Margaret Cunnings was right, he was the handsomest man in the territory. She remembered that day two years ago when Chance took her hand in marriage. It was still almost a fairytale to her, but it was real. It was hard to imagine Chance McCord settling down with a preacher's daughter, but seems the cowboy found something in that pretty little blonde gal that no one else had and wasn't about to let her get away. It was Charity who never thought that the sheriff would be interested in a gal like her. It was as if by accident they met. She was on her way out of the store and Chance was walking in.

Of course, neither had planned what had happened next. Charity not looking where she was going and carrying three large packages walking out of the door of the store and right into the sheriff. Well, as one could guess, they both fell and the packages were scattered all over. Chance, of course, being the gentleman he was, helped her up and insisted on carrying her packages for her. Well, that led to a Sunday luncheon, then a dance and soon an engagement. Before one knew it, the sheriff was a married man.

The sound of Tim Cummings' voice calling for Chance sent everyone looking toward the store. Tim sees Chance and runs over to him holding a piece of paper in his hand. Reaching Chance, he hands him the paper, "this just came in over the wire. I tell you Chance, this is terrible."

Chance looks at the paper and his face grows white. He looks over to the reverend, hands him the paper and steps away.

Charity looks at her father, "what's wrong Papa?"

The reverend clears his throat and in a low voice reads the wire, "On June 25, General George Custer and his men were massacred along the Rosebud River in a place called the Little Big Horn. There were no survivors."

The muffled cries of those who had gathered around were heard and Charity herself had tears rolling down her face. She looks across to her husband who is standing by the horses and begins to walk to him when her father stops her, "let him be right now, he needs to be alone with his thoughts." She looks toward him one more time, then walks away.

Chance looks up as the reverend and Tim walks over to him, "Son, I'll have the church open, so the town folk can gather and perhaps we can tell them what happened."

Chance looks at him, "Andrew, would you tell the folks? I will have to do something and well, it has to be done now."

"Yes of course, but what is so important…"

He looked at Andrew, "I have to save two loves sir."

Chance looks at Tim, "can you get Walker saddled and bring him to the office?"

"I'm on it Chance."

Chance looks at Andrew, "I need to get to Buck and Laughing Eyes before anyone else does. It's not safe for them right now."

Andrew nods he understood. "Do what you have to do Son. We'll take care of things here."

His first stop was at the Lucky Shamrock where the family was getting ready for breakfast when Mick sees Chance ride up. "It's Uncle Chance, it's Uncle Chance!" He runs out of the dining room and towards the front door followed by his father. "Uncle Chance, are you having breakfast with us?"

Trace looks at the man and knows something is wrong, "Mick, let Uncle Chance get off his horse and he'll tell you why he's here."

The boy stepped back and looked at his father. He stepped back, but Chance got off his horse and picked the boy in his arms," you know Mick, you're getting bigger each time I see you."

The smile came back to the boy's face as the three of them walk into the house. Katherine had already poured a cup of coffee for him and she takes Mick from his arms so he can sit down.

Tom smiles at him, "so Chance, what brings you here? Are you looking for these two?" He points to Trace and Shayleen. "Seems they over slept," he cleared his throat on that comment.

Chance smiled, "I understand I had the same problem a few days ago." He looks at Trace and smiles. Then he looks back at Tom. "What I came out her for was to tell you some bad news, seems eight days ago in a place called Little Big Horn, General Custer and his men were killed by the Indians." Before anyone could ask the question, Chance finished, "there were no survivors."

Katherine bowed her head. Tom looked down and uttered, "may God have mercy on their souls."

It was Shayleen who looked at all of them, "Well I for one do not feel sorry for him. He got what he deserved, he didn't give those women and children a chance or even showed any mercy to them at Washita!"

Katherine looked at her, "Shayleen, what about those innocent men?"

"I don't care Katherine, he murdered women and children, they never had a chance! They were told they could stay on that land. They were told they would he safe. Safe until they found gold, then the land was no longer offered to them. Was the gold worth more than the lives of those people? It was the same with the Sand Creek Massacre, in that one Chivington was hailed as a hero, yet he killed women and children and old men. Some hero." She runs out of the room and heads for the stairs and upstairs.

Tom looks at Chance, "she'll be alright, you know how the lass gets. What would be needing form us?"

Mick looks at his grandmother, "why is mommy crying?"

Katherine quietly takes him and the twins into the kitchen, so the men can talk. Chance looks at Trace, "I need your help to get Buck and Laughing Eyes to a safe place until all this is blow over."

"Do you think Buck is in danger? Why he's lived here all his life."

"I know that, but Laughing Eyes hasn't and she is the daughter of a Thunder Sky and right now, that is not too safe around here."

Tom had to agree, Chance was right, "I see we must act fast as soon as news gets around about Custer, no one with any Indian in them is safe." He looks to Trace, "what about the line shack?"

Chance looks at Trace, "line shack?"

"It's a small cabin Buck and I stumbled on a few years back."

"Is it far from here?"

"We could get there in a few hours and it's pretty isolated."

Chance smiles, "perfect."

Tom says, "well let's get things started. What do you need?"

Chance looks at him, "Well Tom, I was kinda hoping you'd stay here at the ranch. I'd feel better of you were here with Katherine and Irish."

Tom thought about it for a moment, then agreed. "Well, at least let me pack some supplies for them."

Trace looks at them, "well looks like I'd better go up and talk to Irish."

Tom looks at him, "good luck on that one Son."

He heads out of the room and up the stairs. He gets to the bedroom door and gently knocks. When Shayleen doesn't answer. he opens the door and sees her siting on the bed. He sees she's been crying. "Autumn?"

She looks up at him. "Don't you dare start on me Trace Cooper. You know very well I'm right. That man killed women and children who never done anything to him or anyone else. He...He..."

"Autumn, listen to me!" He puts his hands on her shoulders. She looks at him. "Chance and I have to go away for a few days."

"Go away? Where? When do we start?"

He smiles down a her, "Well Chance and me have to take Buck and Laughing Eyes away from here for a while. Just until this whole Custer thing settles down. Now as for you my dear wife, you are not going, but you will stay here like a good wife tending to our children. You do remember those three downstairs who call you mommy?"

She gets up off the bed, "Trace Cooper!!"

"Autumn, I mean it you are staying put this time. I'll only be a few days."

She sits back down on the bed and crosses her arms across her chest. But Trance knows that look too well. He knew the moment he and Chance left; she'd be right behind them. "Autumn, I want your promise you'll stay put."

She looks at him, "It's not right. Look why can't they stay here? They would be safe here."

"Chance wants them far enough away that no one will find them. He knows what he's doing. We have to trust him."

She looks up at him, "but they'll be alone."

"They'll have each other, it's all we ever needed, remember?"

She remembered, remembered all too well. Her thoughts went to the scared Buck who tried to muster up the courage to ask Thunder Sky for his daughter's hand in marriage. He had fallen in love with her the first time he saw her and it took three years for him to ask. Tom was so happy, he gave them a hundred acres of land, fifty head of cattle to start their own ranch. He looked on Buck almost as a son and wanted the newlyweds to have a start in life.

It was only last week Laughing Eyes told Shayleen she was expecting a baby. She told her not to tell anyone since she didn't tell Buck yet. Suddenly, she was brought back to the present when there is a knock on the door.

"Irish, may I come in?" Slowly, Chance opens the door and smiles, "I'm not interrupting anything, am I?"

Trace smiles, "no, but maybe you could talk some sense into this stubborn woman."

Chance walks over and stoops down by Shayleen, "I know you want to help and I know you are a good rider, but well, tell you the truth, I need a favor and the only one I can really trust to do it is you."

Her eyes grew wide with excitement, "what is it?"

"Well, I need you to take care of Charity and the baby. Now I know you think it's not so important, but truth is Irish, there ain't anyone I could trust to take care of them. I mean her ma and pa have the town folk to tend to and well, I would feel a lot better if I knew she was here on the ranch with you."

She looks into his eyes, from the first day she met him, she was in love with him. He was her knight in shining armor and was always there for her. How could she say no to his request? There would be a part of her that loved him always. "Alright we'll take Charity and the baby back with us after service."

Chance smiled and picked Shayleen off the bed and kissed her forehead, "love ya Irish." With that he walks out of the room, but stops to look at Trace, "let's not give her a change her mind." With that he was out the door.

Trace takes her on his arms and holds her close, "I need you to be strong for both of us. Remember our spirits will always be together. If you call out my name, I will hear you no matter a where you are."

She looked at him, "you will be careful, promise me.:

He smiled at her, "I'll be careful ma'am, I promise you." He looks into her eyes, "I always said a man could lose his soul in those eyes and I lost mine the day I met you."

With Shayleen and the family standing on the porch, Trace is saying goodbye to the children, then Tom and Katherine until he came to Shayleen, "I'll tell Buck and Laughing Eyes you send your love." He kisses her cheek, "I love you Autumn Sky."

"You come back soon."

Chance hands Trace his horse's reins and tips his hat to Shayleen.

"You take of yourself Chance."

"I will Irish."

With that, they ride off. The others went inside, only Shayleen stood on the porch long after they were out of sight.

~~~~~~

Buck Matthews was walking toward his barn when he saw Laughing Eyes waving to two riders. He thought they were Chance and Trace. Suddenly, shots rang out and Buck was hit. He fell and Laughing Eyes screams and begins running toward him as the riders continue shooting. Her only thought was to get to Buck. A round of bullets rang out this time they hit Laughing Eyes. She falls to the ground yet continues to try to reach Buck. dragging her body, she crawls toward her husband knowing if they are to die, they would be together.

The riders, satisfied they had done their deed rode off, back toward town.

Buck crawled his way toward the lifeless body of his wife. Her eyes looked up at the sky, yet she no longer would see the sunlight of the day. Her body was covered in blood where the bullets had torn through her flesh, leaving only the stain of blood all around the wounds. He
~~~~~~

took her hand in his as he lay beside her, praying he would join her soon. It was there laying in the field that Trace and Chance found him.

It was later in the afternoon when Shayleen and the family had made it in town and to the church. Compared to the early morning bustle, the town had taken on a somber tone, especially upon hearing the news of Custer.

Inside the church, many had gathered to sit, some to pray, and though it was not a formal service, all were welcomed to come in. The reverend felt some would simply like to sit with their neighbors. Though no one knew all the details, the one thing that was certain was there were no survivors.

The door of the church opened and two of Josh Blackthorne's men came in and walked over to him. The taller of the two leaned down and spoke to Blackthorne who nodded and smiled.

The reverend turned and began to speak, "friends, we were saddened to hear of the great loss a few days ago, but let's not let anger take the place of what we know is not the course to take. "

Blackthorne rose from his seat and looked around the room. "I don't know about you folks, but I've given my men orders to shoot any red savage they see. We all have the right to protect ourselves. "

Around the room, many of the townspeople were nodding their heads in agreement. The reverend looks around and feeling the hatred growing. "Friends, do not seek vengeance here. That is not the answer! The good Lord told us to forgive those who persecute us."

Blackthorne looks at him, "well you forgive them Padre, that's your job. As for me, I'm not turning the other cheek. "

Suddenly, the door opens and Shayleen and her family walk in. Margaret gets up and helps with the twins and leads Shayleen and the others to the end row of seats. As they make the way past Blackthorne, Josh nods at Tom as he continues his opinion, "like I was saying, we're not safe while those Injuns are running free. Why there's no telling when they'll get together and attack any of us. Do you realize they killed over two hundred men! Are we gonna let them get away with this?"

~~~~~~~

From the other side of the room, a woman gasps and all eyes look to the back of the church. There standing with Chance's help is a bloody Buck Matthews. The anger in Chance's eyes spoke more than words could ever convey.

Tom walks over to them and helps Chance get him to sit in a nearby pew. He looks at Buck, "Sweet mother Mary, what happened Son?"

A woman in the nearby pew screams as all eyes look at the door where Trace is standing carrying the lifeless body of Laughing Eyes.
~~~~~~~

Shayleen rushes to him and he looks at her with tears in his eyes, "I'm sorry Autumn, we didn't get there soon enough." Shayleen looks at the body of the young woman who was excited at being a mother, she had so much to be grateful for. The anger began to grow in Shayleen. Her friend and her unborn child were killed for no other reason than they were Cheyenne. Gently, she touched her face, then turns and looks at Blackthorne, the anger on her face was directed right to him. "How dare you stand here in the house of God spouting such lies? This man and woman did nothing to you. My God, you all know Buck! He never did anything to hurt you!"

"Now you listen here young lady."

Her eyes were pure fire right now. "No, you listen to me, this woman was my sister. She did nothing wrong to you or anyone else in this town. The only thing wrong, she was Cheyenne. And let me tell you something, you sanctimonious wind bag, Custer was the butcher. He slaughtered women and children at Washita. He attacked the village at dawn. He ordered all be killed. His men killed Black Kettle and his wife as Black Kettle was holding the American Flag. The flag given to him by the president, when he told him the land they were on was theirs's. Did everyone forget that? They were killed on their own land!!!! Oh and let's not forget that great hero Colonel Chivington, who killed so many blood thirsty savages at Sand Creek. Oh wait, they were old men, women and children. I seem to see a pattern here. The whites kill all the woman and children who can't defend themselves and when the braves fight them in battle, they are considered savages."

She looks around the room and all eyes are on her. "You all are ready to kill these savages, as you call them for killing these innocent men, but can you condone doing just what you are talking about doing now? I have never been so ashamed of all of you at this moment. I came back here because I love this land, my children were born here, but I will not let them be raised where a person is judged by the color of his skin, not what is in his soul. Maybe you should search inside that faith you talk so much about and remember even Jesus forgave those who nailed him the cross. "

She turns and Blackthorne smirks, "you would talk that way, you married an Indian lover. "

She turned around and with all the force she had she smacked his face. The sound of the crack was heard across the room. "You're just lucky you are in the house of the Lord, don't let me forget that. "

She walks back to Trace as he smiles at her. His Autumn fought like a warrior in front of the town. She looks at him, "let's go home. "They walk out of the church followed by Tom, Katherine and the children, Margaret and Tim.

Tom and Katherine and the children, and Chance. It's Trace who helps Buck get in the wagon and Tom helps

Trace put Laughing Eyes in the back. Chance, Trace and Shayleen get in Buck's wagon and Tom takes Charity in their wagon. The wagons start out of town with Margaret and Tim following behind. As the wagons move along, Chance notices the towns folk pointing to them. He looks at Shayleen and smiles, "Well Irish I got to say it, you managed to get everybody's attention with your little ruckus at the church. "

"Oh come on Chance, don't tell me you didn't want to punch him?" He looked down and smiled, he had to admit he did. She knew it didn't matter, nothing would bring Laughing eyes back.

<center>~~~~~~~~</center>

It was dark by the time Shayleen, Trace and Chance got to the spirits place. It was agreed that this would be the best place to have Laughing Eyes service. Here where the spirits would come and bring her spirit and soul with her ancestors. Trace and Chance gathered the branches and stones to rest her body on. Slowly, he placed her body on the bed of branches' and as Shayleen handed him the torch, he began to light the branches around the woman's body.

Both Shayleen and Trace watched the flames consume her body sending streams of white smoke above them and up to the spirits that would lead her to their ancestors. Shayleen placed her hand in Traces as he looks down and in a low voice he says, "I promised our father I would take care of her. I told him she would be safe living here with us and no harm would come to her. How do I tell him she's dead? How can I tell him she was killed because she was Cheyenne?" He looked at Shayleen, "what will happen now? What will happen to all the Cheyenne? Will they as well as the others be destroyed and forgotten, never to be spoken about again?"

She looks at him trying to hold back the tears, "we won't let them be forgotten Trace. We can't let all this violence go unheard of. We will find a way to let their voices be heard."

Chapter 2

As August came, news of Colorado's statehood spread throughout the land as celebrations were being scheduled. At the Lucky Shamrock, Buck Matthews was progressing nicely with the healing of his wounds under the care of Tom and Katherine. Each day his strength was returning and though he smiled at times, he also was plagued with the memory of losing the women he loved. Each time Shayleen saw him with Mick and the girls, her heart ached for the fact he was denied his own child to love.

Life around the ranch had begun to return to normal, it was clear that it was the rock Shayleen held on to for strength. Here were all the memories of happier times, and no matter what happened anywhere else, The Lucky Shamrock would always be a safe haven for whatever life had in store for her. During these past months Shayleen spent so much time trying to sort out the good and the bad of what happened and still asked the question why? She sat in her office keeping a journal of all that had happened leading up to Custer's death and the events after. She had promised Trace, the Cheyenne would not be forgotten nor would their heritage. She looked up from her journal as Trace walked in the room, and puts his hands on her shoulders, "are you busy?"

"No. just going over all that has happened and writing down the events."

He walks over to the window and gazes outside, looking at nothing in particular. He worries about his wife and searches for a way to bring her back to the Shayleen he knew. "There's a celebration in town."

She answers with no attention to the conversation. "That's nice."

"Well, I was thinking we could all go and have a good time."

'She puts down her pen and looks at him, "I really have so much to do here Trace, but you could go with the children."

He looks at her, "Autumn, you have to let it go! It's been over two months since Laughing Eyes was killed. It's time to move on!"

When she looked at him. "Killed? Trace, she was murdered because she was an Indian. That was the reason the fine people of this brand-new state felt the reason to murder his woman. A woman who posed no threat to them, yet they felt it was their need to murder her! I'm sorry Trace, but I don't think there is really anything to celebrate at this time."

He walks over to her and picks her up off the chair, "Autumn, you have shut yourself up in this house so long you don't even know your family anymore!"

She looks at him, "I don't want to discuss this."

He looks into her eyes, he wanted to see that fire he knew she had, yet she only looked at him with a cold stare, "We will discuss this and it will be done now. It's time you listened to some reason." He opens the door and starts heading down the hall where they see Tom and Buck.

Shayleen pleads to her father for help, "Papa, tell him to let me go."

Tom smiles and looks at Trace, "watch your back Son and don't let her get that hand free."

He smiled at Tom, "I won't Pop"

'Tom and Buck walk back into the kitchen and smile.

Buck looks at him, "you think Trace's scheme will work Tom?"

"It's hard to say, but I know Trace and I know he'll do anything for me girl."

"Yea, but you know Irish, she's a stubborn one."

"That she is Buck, but you know Trace can be just as stubborn."

Shayleen rode in silence as Trace leads her horse, since he had her hands tied to the saddle horn. He didn't look back once at her, yet he could feel he eyes burning into his back. He watched her for the past two months build a wall around her and the while family. Never leaving that office from early morning to the late hours of the night. She had turned herself away from everyone, even the children. All he wanted was to have his Autumn back, only he didn't know how to do it.

They finally reached the clearing that led to the path to the Spirits Place, he remembered he had taken her here when Tom was shot. They had spent many nights under the stars here, it was a special place to them. As he walks over to untie her hands, he looks up at her. "I want your promise that you won't try to run."

"Run? Where would I go?"

He unties her hands from the saddle horn and helps her off the horse. He looks at her, "come on, you know the way as well as I do. "

She starts out and in a few minutes, they reach the stream. It's just as she remembers, beautiful and peaceful. It truly was the most beautiful place on earth.

He glanced at her for a moment and thought he saw a spark of his Autumn, that spark of life that had been gone since Laughing Eyes died. He knew the pain she was feeling, he also knew that somehow, someway, he had to make her see she had to come back. He looked at her, "do you remember the first time you were here?"

She looked at him, "it was when Papa was shot. You took me here to think."

He smiled at her, "well it's time you need to think again Sweetheart."

"Trace I don't..."

He takes her hands in his and looks at her. "Make the time! You can't let this eat at you. It will destroy you and I can't sit back and watch it destroy the woman I love so much. Sweetheart you are in a dark place right now and it's not where you should be. It will destroy you." He sees the tears in her eyes and pulls her close to him. The pain and sorrow she had held inside of her all these months finally was emerging. Sobs, sorrow and anger all melted together with the tears.

"Let it all out Autumn Sky, come back to this life."

Her sobs were soft at first, then they grew louder. He held her until the sun began to fall behind the mountain and the evening dusk began to roll in. He gently sets her down as he begins to gather wood for the campfire. He lights the fire and looks over to Shayleen, the glow from the fire gave a warm tone to her face, he could see she was coming back. He had been able to reach her. Quietly, they sat by the fire. Trace looks over at her. The anger and sadness was almost gone, she had let the process of healing begin.

As they look into the flames of the campfire, they hear the cry of a wolf. "He sounds so lonely, almost like he's lost his mate," she said in a mournful tone.

He takes her hand in his and gently squeezes it. "I almost lost mine, but she came back to me."

Gently, she kisses his hand, then his cheek, "I'm sorry I caused you to worry Running Wolf."

"I always worry about you Autumn, I have from the from the first day I saw you." He takes her in his arms and holds her close as they continue to sit by the fire without saying a word. She is content to know Trace is there for her. Here in this small secluded space hidden from the outside world time seemed to stop and the healing of all sorrows began.

~~~~~~

Tom and Katherine were up early the next morning. The twins, contented in their chairs waiting to be fed as Buck comes in the room with Mick on his back as if Buck is the horse. As he walks by Katherine at the stove he stops. "Is that bacon I smell Katherine?"

She smiles at him, "I seemed to remember it is your favorite. "

He smiles as he steals a piece from the plate she is holding and he makes his way to the table. He looks at Tom. "Do you think Trace and Irish will be heading back today?"

Tom passes him a cup of coffee, "hard to say Son, you know how stubborn me lass can be."

Buck smiles knowing how true that was, "that's true."

Trace awakens finding Shayleen standing near the stream. In the early morning, the view was breathtaking. He walks up to her and puts his arms around her and holds her close. "Good morning."
~~~~~~

She smiles and turns to him, "morning."

"Feeling better today?"

She nods and looks into his eyes, "Trace, promise me something?"

"If I can."

"Promise nothing will change in this spot. Promise me it will always stay like this."

As he looked into her eyes, he knew he would give her the world and more, he never could refuse her, yet there was no guarantee this spot would never change. "I'll do my best, that's all I can promise you, but I will promise you as long as I am alive, it will never change. But remember as long as we hold this memory in our minds it will never disappear from our minds or hearts."

She put her arms around his neck and looks at him, "as long as I have you in front of me, I need nothing else in my lifetime."

He looks at her, "maybe we can or at least let people know what happened to the Cheyenne."

She looked at him, "I started a journal when Buck and I were snowed in at the cabin four years ago. Buck curled up by the fire and slept, I started writing and just kept writing. In the morning, I put the journal in my saddle bag and it's been in the closet back home ever since."

He smiled at her and kissed her, "Autumn, you are beautiful. Come on, we have to get home."

It was mid-afternoon when Tom saw Trace and Shayleen coming up the trail toward the house. "Katherine, Buck, children, come quick, Trace and Shayleen are home!"

The door flung open and Mick runs out and heads toward his parents. Katherine and Buck come out on the porch, each holding one of the twins. With tears in her eyes, she smiles, her prayers were answered. She looks at Tom, "he did it Tom. IIe got our little girl back."

Tom moves toward Katherine and puts his arm around her shoulder, "that he did Katherine, that he did." Tom smiled as he watched as Trace grabbed Mick and swung him in the saddle with him and smiled at the others.

Shayleen looked at them all and smiled, something they had missed seeing her do for a while. It was Tom who helped her down from the horse and hugged her. She gave Katherine a hug and then walked over to Buck, "I'm ready to be Irish again." She hugs him and smiles and smiles at Trace. It was Katherine who decided to get everyone back inside, "well I don't know about you people, but I can tell you three little ones are hungry and I'm sure Buck is about ready to eat, so let's all get inside and eat." Slowly, they all file in and head for the dining room where the table is set.

Later that evening, Trace is busily searching in the bedroom closet for the saddle bag with the journal in it. As Shayleen sits quietly on the chair, she watches the contents of the closet being flung out the closet door and wondering who will clean it up. "Sweetheart, I love you dearly and don't get me wrong, but are you sure you put this journal in the closet?" He stuck his head out the door, "of course, I'm sure." She heard a loud thump and then, "At last!" Trace came out with the leather book in his hands, "I told you it was here." He handed it to her and smiled. "You can be the first to read it my dear."

She opens the book and reads the dedication. '*To my Autumn Sky who is my world and my life I give her these words to let others know the true story of the Cheyenne people and to let others know the injustices done to them.*' She looks at him with tears in her eyes and begins to read. '*With all the events that had happened I wanted to put this down so all people will know the true story. The Cheyenne people were proud people, they never wanted war. Their chief Black Kettle wanted all to live in peace. In August of 1864, he signed a peace treaty with the whites. He believed the white man would honor it. He thought like the Cheyenne, a man's word was his honor. Three months later, Colonel. Chivington and his men attacked the village and killed 123 Cheyenne, mostly women and children. Seems the white man's word had no honor. It was during this attack, Black Kettle and his wife Medicine Women were injured, they were saved by hiding in the banks along the river. It was Black Kettle who took his people, what was left of them and headed north and settled again in an area called Washita. Again, the land was promised to the Cheyenne. Once again, the white father promised they would not be sent off the land. With Chivington in Colorado, a new demon had come to the west. A brash young man, a boy general he was called. He made a name for himself in the Civil War and was now on his way to glory out in the west., The man was Custer, George Armstrong Custer. With his flashy uniform and golden locks, he did seem a bit out of place in the west. With the discovery of gold in the hills, it was the prospectors who urged the government to have the army protect them from the savages. The savages that were on their land. Land given to them by the government that now wants them moved off. And so, on November 26,1868, the Seventh Calvary, led by Custer in the early hours of the morning did attack and slaughter the entire village. Black Kettle and his wife were killed as they stood facing the horses, charging at them. Black Kettle was struck down and killed still holding the American Flag. Both he and his wife's bodies were then trampled on by the soldiers' horses, until they were barely recognizable. The man who had only sought peace, lay dead with the rest of his people, as the village was left in a pile of dead bodies and ashes.'*

As Shayleen read the words, she remembered Thunder Sky with great fondness. She remembered his smile when she and Trace were married at his village. Her thoughts were then on Laughing Eyes, the shy young girl who was more sister to her than if she had been of the same parents.

She looked at Trace as she closed the book, "someday this story will be told, I promise you. Somehow I will make sure the Cheyenne as well as the other tribes will have their voices heard."

Later that evening, Shayleen stood by the window of their bedroom as the sun began to sink behind the mountain. She stood and wondered how could all this be happening. How can the west she knew destroy so many innocent lives in the name of progress? It seemed progress was just another word for taking what belongs to someone else. To put it simply, it was another word for stealing. She was still determined to supply Thunder Sky's people with food and blankets for the approaching winter. It was a promise Tom had made to Trace and she planned to keep it. At least it would be said, the O'Malley family kept their word. Still looking out the window, she didn't hear Trace come into the room. He walks up behind her and takes her in his arms. She turns and looks at him, "Trace, they are trying to destroy these people."

He looks at her, "they will always have their spirit Autumn. You'll never let them forget that. You are part of them as much as I am." He looks into her eyes, how many times he had said, he had lost his soul in them. Yet each time he saw the passion and fire in them. he loved her more. Gently he leans down and kisses her. She softly moans as his lips move from her lips to her throat. Suddenly he picks her up in his arms and carries her to bed, once there, his kisses down her body and sends shivers up and down her spine. Slowly, he undresses her sending a fire throughout her body. Trace looked down into her eyes and gently kissed her lips as their fire began to stir again. He continued to run a trail of kisses up her neck until, he reaches her lips. "Shayleen Cooper, you are a woman of great passion in everything you do."

She looked at him, "In all I do?"

He pulls her closer to him, "most definitely in everything you do."

Slowly, her body under his skilled hands became a bed of.

It was an early morning a month later, when Mick aroused all in the house to come out to see his surprise. It was true the boy had been keeping a secret for all this time with sneaking off each afternoon with Buck, but no one seemed to know the big secret. That is until that morning. As they all gathered by the corral, Buck opened the barn door and there sat Mick on top of a full-size horse.

Shayleen stood up on the fence only to have Trace push her back down again. With Buck close by, Mick put the horse through the paces of walking around the corral. Each time he passed the group, the smiles on their faces told the boy they were pleased. When his show was over, everyone ran over to congratulate him, everyone, but Shayleen. She did try, but she was overcome with a feeling of dizziness, then she stumbled and fell. Katherine was the first to get to her. 'Shayleen!!"

Trace reaches them and picks Shayleen up in his arms and rushes her into the house.

Tom looks Buck "get into town and get the doc."

Katherine and Tom rush into the house with the twins and Mick. Upstairs in their bedroom, Trace has laid Shayleen on their bed and holds her hand, waiting for her to regain conscience. Katherine rushes in with a cloth "Trace, why don't you wait downstairs? Buck went to get the doctor. I think I…"

She looks at him, the last thing she needed now was to have him under her feet. "Trace, Tom needs help with the little ones and you need to tell Mick everything is alright"

"He looks at Shayleen, still unresponsive. "Go on now, I'll call for you the moment she awakens."

The doc arrived and was taken upstairs which seems like hours ago. Trace stood at the foot of the stairs ready to run up at the first call, yet the wait continued. It was early evening when the doctor came down to see Trace sitting on the bottom step. Hearing the footsteps on the stairs, he jumps up and turns to him. "Doc?"

The old man smiles at Trace, "she's gonna be alright Trace."

"But she fainted and…"

"Well, sometimes that happens to women in the early stages of pregnancy."

Trace looks at the old man who has smile on his face, "don't worry Son, she'll be fine and in about six months she'll be back to normal again."

"Can I go see her Doc?"

He old man smiles, "of course you can go on up, Katherine needs a break about now."

Trace smiles and races up the stairs. In the bedroom Katherine is fixing the covers as Trace rushes in. He looks at his Autumn, sitting up in bed looking pale, but her smile lights up the room. He walks over and kisses her forehead, "you gave us all a scare."

She smiles at him, "Well, it's kinda a shock for me too."

Katherine looks at them, "I'm going down to check on the rest of the brood now, you two behave yourselves."

Trace smiles and puts his hand up, "oh I will, it's just Autumn is the one who causes trouble."

She gives a gentle punch as Katherine shakes her head and heads out the door.

He looks at her as Katherine closes the door. "What was this, I heard you're having another child?"

"Well, as I remember, it does require two people to make a little one. Therefore, I should rephrase that statement and say we're expecting another child."

He had to admit she was, as usual, right. But that still didn't give her the right to give him a scare. She makes a move to get up and he places her back down on the pillows. "Trace, it's only a baby and I have had three, you know the three young ones running around downstairs."

He looks at her, "none the less, you will stay in bed and rest for the rest of the day."

She smiles at him, "seems staying in bed caused this problem."

Tom comes up and gently knocks on the bedroom door. Shayleen by now in bed in the room was glad to have the company. He opens the door and smiles at her. "How are yee feeling Lass?"

"Oh I'm fine Papa, it's Trace who insists I stay in bed."

Tom smiles at her, "well he's right, you could be having twins again. Besides, it's time you let go some of the load."

She looks at him, "Papa, everything is alright, isn't it?"

"Why sure it is Lass, everything is fine." He leans down and kisses her forehead and turns to walk out of the room.

~~~~~~
~~~~~~

Aa the days passed into months, it became evident that Shayleen was with child and this was not an easy pregnancy for her. Plagued with morning sickness the entire day, the smell of food cooking sent her to her bed until the waves of nausea subsided. There were times she refused to come down from her room for days and when she did come down, she was as pale as a white sheet. It was Trace who put his foot down, forbidding her to even think of riding until after the baby was born.

About three months before Shayleen was due, Buck decided to it was time for him to head for Oklahoma and find Thunder Sky. He had not seen the man since his marriage to Laughing Eyes. He felt he was ready now to tell him what had happened to his daughter. It was something he needed to do to give peace to his soul. As the family gathered to say goodbye to Buck. Katherine was the first to give him a hug, "I want you to be careful. And remember to come back home to us. It just won't be the same without you here." Her voice cracks as she hides her tears. He walks over to Tom, "I'm giving yee my best horse Son. Make sure you give Thunder Sky our best and as soon as Lassie here has her young'un, we'd be making the trip to see him."

He comes up to Trace, who gives him and hug, "You watch out in your travels Brother, stay safe and come back as soon as you can."

He smiles as he reaches Shayleen, "seems I've saved the best for last. Irish, you take care of yourself, you are a special woman, Autumn Sky and don't let anyone tell you different. You are the sister I would have been proud to have and the friend I cherish in my life."

He hugs her she holds back the tears. "You would have to go now when I'm gonna have a baby in two months and well, we'd like him to know his uncle Buck. He looks at her and for moment, just looks into her eyes. He had always loved her and always would, until the end of his days. He looks at Trace again as he hands him the reins of the horse, "ride safe my brother." He mounts the horse and turns to them all and waves as he rides off. As they all go in, Shayleen stays in the porch until Buck is out of sight.

Months later, Matthew Sky Cooper was born. He was named for Buck and Thunder Sky, it was Shayleen's wish.

Tom and Trace felt a celebration was in order since another male was in the house. At the early age of three weeks, he displayed his mother's temper and her raven hair. It was Chance who stood in for Buck as the baby's godfather had to admit the boy was all his mother. It was Tom who looked at his daughter as she held her new baby in her arms. He was pleased at how her life had become. Why she was married to a fine man, had four beautiful children and was well respected by the townsfolk.

~~~~~~
~~~~~~

In 1891, just eighteen miles from Colorado Springs, gold was found at Cripple Creek. It was on the side of Pikes Peak and was said the richest strike was found. Some say it was richer than Sutters Mill. It wasn't long before every man with a dream was heading to Cripple Creek.

Overnight, mining towns cropped up and it soon became a need for supplies to accommodate the miners. Bob Womack was a supplier for the mining company who knew the easiest way to keep the miners up in the hills was to have the supplies freighted up to them. He also heard a friend of his, Trace Cooper was living in Colorado Springs. He had known Trace in his younger days and knew the man knew the mountain trails as good, if not better than any white man. They may be a chance he could have him transport the supplies to the mining camps. Though the money Womack offered was tempting, it would mean Trace would be away from home more than he liked. With Autumn getting back on her feet and branding time on the ranch, it just could not be done. He needed ranch hands for the branding, yet everyone was heading up the mountain to dig for gold. No, he would have to turn down Womack's offer.

As he rides up to the ranch, he sees Tom sitting on the porch. His first thought was to ask Tom's advice on the offer. As he got closer, he noticed Tom was sleeping and decided to let him rest. Trace smiled, he had grown to love the man like he was his own father. He was glad he had taken both Autumn and his advice to slow down and enjoy the children in his later years. After all these years he should be able to enjoy his grandchildren. He quietly passes by him and walks into the house where he runs into Shayleen.

She smiles at him, "I'm glad you're here. I was just going to call Papa in for supper. Now you can do it."

"He's sleeping. He looks so peaceful; I hate to wake him."

A chill ran through her spine as she raced outside to her father's side. "Papa, Papa," she tries shaking him, but no response. "Trace come here quickly!"

Trace rushes out the door and to her side, as she keeps trying to wake him. It was no use, he was gone. The little Irishman had gone to join his beloved Colleen. Never more would she hear him call for his Lass.

News traveled fast about Tom's passing and Chance and Charity were the first to arrive with Reverend Williams. Tim and Margaret closed the store and came out to be with Katherine and Shayleen as arrangements were being made. The blow was equally hard for Margaret, who after losing her own father was lucky enough to have Tom fill in and take his place. He had loved her as if she were his daughter. While Katherine bravely greeted visitors at the door, thanking them for coming, Shayleen stayed in er room, shutting the world out and keeping her grief private.

It was Charity who went upstairs to see her. She gently tapped on the door waiting for a response and walked in, shutting the door behind her. Slowly, she walked closer to her, "I came up here to see how you are."

She looked at her, "I'm fine Charity. I want to thank you and your parents for all your help these past few days. It means a great deal to me and Katherine.

Charity sits down beside her and takes her hand in hers, "It was our pleasure to help out." She started to say something, then hesitated, then started again, "there is something I wanted to ask you, and maybe this is not the right time, but… I always wanted you and I to have the same friendship Trance and Chance have. I always felt you resented me after all you and Chance…"

Shayleen stops her, "Charity, whatever you may have thought it's not true. Chance is so happy and that makes me happy. Make no mistake, I do love him and always will, but it's not the same love I have for Trace or the love Chance has for you."

"Thank you for telling me this."

Shayleen looked at her, "I should have told you a long time ago."

Suddenly, there was a knock on the door and Chance and Trace walked in, Chance walks over to his wife and kisses her forehead, "is this a private party or can anyone join?"

Shayleen looks at him, "well that all depends, did you bring anything up."

Chance smiles at Trace who takes from behind his back, a fine botte of bourbon.

"I believe m lady does like this type of refreshment." He hands her the bottle while he grabs four glasses from the nearby table. He smiles at Chance, "I always believe in being prepared." They toasted to their friendship, their health and their children.

The next morning beside Shayleen stood Trace and Katherine as they watched Chance, Tim's ranch hands take Tom to his final resting place. Everyone had come to pay their respects; the little man was well liked.

As the reverend stated the Lords's Prayer, the others soon followed in. After the service, everyone gathered back at the ranch, It had always been a place of such happy occasions one almost expected to see Tom walk in the room at any point.

Katherine, Lord love her was a tower of strength as she sat with Shayleen's twins beside her on the floor. It was Trace who came up to them, "girls, have you seen Mama?" They look at each other, then back to him, "no Papa."

Katherine had that worried look on her face as she looks at Trace, "Trace?"

He looks at her, "don't worry Mama, I'll find her." He sees Chance across the room and tries to get his attention.

He comes over still smiling as not to arise suspicion, "what's wrong Trace?"

"I seemed to have misplaced Autumn; can you stick around until I get back?"

"Sure, but do you want some help?"

"I think have an idea of where she might be. I'll be back as soon as I can." He smiled at Trace, "don't worry about anything, I'll take core of things here."

"Thanks." He heads out the back door and toward the barn. He notices something under the nearby tree. As he gets closer, he sees it's Shayleen. As he walks up to her, he sees she's been crying, "I'm sorry Trace, I just couldn't …"

He gently takes her in his arms and walks her into the barn. Once inside, he holds her gently, "my brave Autumn Sky always trying to be strong for everyone. You're hurting so bad now and you feel you have to be brave. I'm here for you. I'll always be here for you."

She looks up at him, "promise me, promise me you won't ever leave me? I couldn't bear to lose you too. You're all I have to keep me going. I don't want to face life without you Trace."

He looks into her eyes, he wanted to tell her about Cripple Creek and the offer from Womack, but just couldn't. At that moment, all he wanted was to have her in his arms forever and never let her go. His Autumn needed him. He wanted to take away the pain, but he knew he couldn't, but at least knew he could comfort her now. "I promise I won't leave you."

With Tom gone, the ranch was left to run. If he was ever disappointed about not going to Cripple Creek, he never once showed it. Colorado Springs was growing, yet the Lucky Shamrock had the same qualities it had when Tom was there. There was always a smile for a stranger and if they needed a job, one was always there for the asking. Trace had decided to expand and start breeding horses he and Chance formed a partnership where Autumn Sky would handle the horse breeding part, leaving Trace to concentrate on the steers. Since Chance no longer was sheriff, his decision to once again go back to ranching. Trace could think of no other person to partner up with than Chance with the exception of Buck. Yet with Chance purchasing Buck's ode homestead, it was made to seem like he was still there. He even named the place Autumn Sky, in honor of Irish and the partnership he and Trace shared.

It wasn't long before horse buyers from all over the state came to see and buy these fine-looking animals. Of course, the discovery of gold at Cripple Creek sent settlers from all around to Colorado looking to find that dream. New families were moving in each day while others decided to move on. Tim and Margaret Cummings were two of those people. Colorado Springs was home to them; Margaret's folks were the first townsfolk to greet the O'Malley's when they came here. Margaret and

Shayleen were as close as sister's. But when Margaret got the wire her brother, in Denver, had passed leaving his store to her she had to go. Tim even joked saying one day there would be a string of Cummings' mercantile in the state. Besides they were leaving the store here to Timmy. Who just recently married that pretty young Jefferson gal Jenny. Yes, Tim would do good with the store and the folks all knew him. Billy, on the other, had moved in a different circle, he took over Chance's old job and became Deputy Sheriff. Seems all those years hanging in Chance's office paid off. Sixteen-year-old Colleen and Katherine Cooper were on their way with their grandmother to go to Boston to visit Katherine's sisters. Of course, they wanted Shayleen to join them, but she stated she simply could not leave the ranch at this time of year. It was branding time and the steers had to be taken to the rail way.

Yes, things were changing and later that year, Sarah McCord, Chance's little girl married Billy Cummings, the deputy sheriff and the boy who hung around the sheriff's office as a kid. Chance couldn't be happier; he had always thought if he had a son he'd want him to be like Billy and now he has him. The whole town had assembled outside the church to witness the ceremony.

As the young couple exchanged their vows Trace looks over to his wife and smiles. One day they will be watching their girls exchange vows and move on to start their new lives. Chance is beaming as he danced with Charity and then hands her over to Billy.

When the music ended, a familiar tune began and Shayleen felt a tap on her shoulder. "I believe this is our song Irish?"

She looks at him knowing it's the same song they danced to the night he told her he loved her. She smiles and puts her hand in his, "I didn't think you'd remembered."

As they gently moved across the dance floor, it was as if they were the only two people dancing. Chance McCord, handsome as he was all those years ago, smiling at the woman he foolishly let slip away. And though he had no regret on marrying Charity, there would always be a special place in his heart for his beloved Irish.

He smiles at her, "I could never forget the night I told you I loved you. I still love you and always will. Why we were dancing to this song."

She smiled up at him, "I love you too, Chance and you'll always be special to me."

Even though they had moved on and married others, each had kept the heart charm they had exchanged that summer so long ago. It was their bond that could never be broken.

As they danced around the floor Shayleen glances at Trace, who smiles at her. It was then that Margaret walked over to Trace and takes his hand, "care to join me

Trace? It doesn't seem right for a handsome guy like you not out there dancing. Come on make an old gal happy."

He smiles and leads her to the dance floor as they begin to begin to dance. They danced by Chance and Shayleen and Margaret smiles ay her, "seems you're not the only one who can find a handsome man."

Trace looks at Shayleen and smiles. "Pardon me ma'am, do I know you?"

She looks at him "why yes, don't you remember, I'm the woman you sleep with."

"Ah yes, I thought I knew the face."

~~~~~~

They all began to laugh and as the music stopped, they returned to the tables. It wasn't till later that Shayleen thought about how did Trace really feel about her dancing with Chance. She sits on the bed as he takes off his shorts and climbs into and smiles at her, "you looked beautiful today as he leans over and kisses her cheek. "Trace?"

"Hum?"

"Trace, did it bother you that I danced with Chance?"

He took her in his arms and smiles at her, "my sweet Autumn Sky, you never have to worry about that. I love you and there is no way I would ever be jealous of you. Chance is special to you and always will be. I also know you love me and that's all that matters. The first day I
~~~~~~

saw you, I knew that I would love you for all my days. You are my heart song and I could never want another but you, my sweet lady." He places his lips on hers and her arms gently go around his neck. She presses her body closer to him and his arms go around her waist as he feels her passion mounting. In a voice just above a whisper she moans his name. Even after all these years, this woman still, had the power to crave more and more. He let out a groan and her tongue began to probe his mouth. It wasn't long before they both lay back completely exhausted. He looked at her, "I'll never stop loving you my lady."

She looked at him, "you'll always be my mountain man." As they settle in each other's arms the drift off to sleep.

Chapter 4

Things were changing for the ranchers. Soon the days of the open range would be gone. Barbed wire was being strung up all over the range. In the name of progress, the ranches of year ago were now just a memory. In 1889, President Harrison passed a bill that opened all land that once belonged to the Indians was now offered to settlers. On April 22, of that year in something called the Oklahoma Land Rush wagons were lined up to get their dream 'land'.

Shayleen threw the paper down in discuss, "when will it end? First, they take the land from the Indians, then they take the children, what next!" My God Trace, they are Cheyenne and should never forget that. They are taking everything from them, even hope."

He looks at her, "you know that's not true; the Cheyenne will never give up their hope."

"Trace, can't you see what they have done? They have broken every treaty and will keep doing it. They give the land that is theirs to begin with, then take it away from them."

"I know."

She gets up and walks over to the door and in a fit of rage, she punches the wall and puts a hole in the wall. "I am not going to sit back and watch this continue."

"Autumn, let's try to calm down," he was concerned about her hand that was bleeding.

She looks at hm, "calm down, dear God in heaven, how can you just sit there and let them do this to our friends?"

He finally grabs her hand gently, he sees nothing is broken, but there is a nasty cut across the wrist. As he manages to calm her down and get her seated again. He hands her a book.

"What's this?"

"It's a book."

She again looks at him, "well I can see that, what am I to do with it?"

"It was written by a women named Helen Johnson, she goes on about how the federal government's treatment of the Indians and people are seeing this all over the country. The word is getting out Autumn, I'm not saying you show what you feel. I just say pick your battles Autumn Sky."

"She looks at him, "how can I pick my battles, no one will listen to me here."

He smiles at her, "read the book, it will show you the way." He kisses her forehead and slowly makes his way out of the room.

~~~~~~
~~~~~~

After the Oklahoma land raid, congress opened up land in Montana. Land that was the land of the Cress and Cherokee, it seemed the word was not getting out fast enough for Shayleen. In these days her thoughts fell on Thunder Sky and though she missed him, she was glad he was not here to see what was happening to his people. She thought of happier times, how a small village opened up their hearts to a young girl who was hurt. Of a young girl who tended to her and because she was Cheyenne was murdered along with the baby she was carrying. Fighting back the tears, she looked out the window. Lord, how she missed them.

Trace walked in the room and looked at her. He always seemed to know what she was thinking and his time was no different, "I miss them too Sweetheart, maybe we can take a trip up to see them after roundup."

She looks at him and smiles, "oh could we Trace? I'd love to see Thunder Sky and Buck."

He leans down and kisses her forehead, "if it will make you happy, we will go, I promise."

~~~~~~

The Lucky Shamrock was getting ready for the event of the season. The Cooper girls were getting married and on the same day. It was always known that the two girls would grow up and leave the ranch, just that no one thought it would be on the same day.
~~~~~~

Katherine Cooper had met Sam Weston in Denver when attending college. Sam's family was in the banking business and young Sam planned to follow in the family business. Though Katherine who was raised on a ranch and was at home on a horse, Sam, well, he was what one would call a city boy. Matter of fact, horses scared him. She had written to her mother that Sam was taking riding lessons in hopes to be ready to ride with the family when he gets to the ranch.

Shayleen smiled when she read that. Her thoughts were not so bright when it came to Colleen. Colleen had a gentle and maybe that's why she fell in love with a man that didn't deserve such a special soul. Lucas Walsh never took life seriously, to him it was live for today and the hell with the tomorrows. He had seen Colleen come out of a local dress shop with Katherine and each carrying numerous packages, he immediately offered to help them carry their purchases for them After all, it was a gentlemanly gesture.

As they walked to the nearby carriage, he introduced himself as Lucas Walsh, who had come out west to purchase horses for his family's ranch in Virginia. It seemed his family was in search of purchasing horses from out west to ultimately have the finest breed of stock in the state. As you may have just already guessed, bumping into the girls was not an accident, he tried to pass it off as. He had been closely watching the girls for the past three days. His pretense at being a gentleman was to gain their confidence and a way to perhaps gain even more.

The first time he met Shayleen and Trace was when he appeared at the ranch stating he was interested in purchasing some horses for his family's ranch in Virginia. He came, prepared with a letter from his father Judge Alexander Walsh stating he gave his son full power to handle any dealings on the matter. Though everything appeared legal. Chance wanted to check it out. He sent a wire to Judge Walsh in Virginia and he did find out the judge did have son who was sent out west to purchase horses to breed with his.

During the two weeks Lucas was at the ranch, he did his best to win over the Coopers, only there was still something that Trace was not sure of. Not to hurt his daughter and with some misgivings, Trace agreed to let Colleen marry him. The entire town and even the governor of the state were invited and attended the wedding. The Weston family arrived three days before while the judge sent his regrets stating he and his wife could not attend due to pressing issues. And so that afternoon, Trace with both his ladies walked down the aisle to become married ladies. The reception went on into the night as the newlyweds were driven into town for some privacy and to start their lives in the morning when they boarded the train back.

~~~~~~
~~~~~~

The ranch seemed quieter now that the girls were gone and Matt was back east, also, in medical school. Mick and his two sons were helping Chance with the horses. Katherine and Sam found a nice small house on the outskirts of town and within walking distant to the bank. Sam's father made him vice president of the bank with a promise of a promotion to president in five years when he retired.

Colleen on the other hand was not so lucky. They never did go back to Virginia; seems Lucas was not all he said he was. Oh, true he was Judge Walsh's son, but the fact of him out west to purchase horse for the judge was not true. Oh, granted, he did start out with that notion and his father did give him the permission for the transactions until the deals began to go sour. It was the third deal he made in a town in Wyoming. Oh, he did have all the intentions of buying the horses for his father and there was an agreement on a fair price, but there was also a fine-looking poker game in the saloon that evening and Lucas always did have a weakness for whisky, women and poker. Well, it seems lady luck found someone else to be with that night and Lucas lost it all the horse money as well his money. He went home and took what little money Colleen had and her grandmother's brooch. It was her grandmother Colleen's. She brought it here from Ireland and had been in the family for years. He looked at the jewel, it had to be worth something after all, it had a gold setting. Besides Lucas needed money. Colleen tried to grab it from him and he pushed her to the floor and proceeded to beat her. He left her on the bedroom floor crying and bleeding from the beating she had endured. It wasn't the first time he had hit her, but this time she was determined it would be her last. Slowly she got up from the floor and cleaned herself up. She had to get out before he came back or he would surely beat her again. She had to make it Aunt Margaret and Uncle Tim's. She knew she would be safe there. She had gone to them before when he was like this.

Back at the saloon Lucas' luck was no better. Losing all the money he had stolen from his wife and what the pin had given him, he was now totally broke. There was no way out for him, he got up from the table and aimed his pistol at the dealer, claiming the dealer was dealing from under the deck. As he fired, three other men fired at him point blank. He stumbled back and fell to the floor dead. It was mid-morning when the sheriff was able to find the where abouts of Mrs. Walsh. It was only after Tim Cummings had heard what had happened in the saloon the night before did Tim tell him where he could find Colleen. He accompanied the sheriff to the house and Margaret proceeded to tell him what had been happening these past four months and the beatings this girl has endured. She also stated that Colleen would be staying with them until other arrangements could be made for her to return to her parents in Colorado Springs. What neither of them knew at the time was she was pregnant. Colleen handled the news of Lucas' death quite well, Margaret seemed to think it was more a relief for her yet it really wasn't something she wanted to tell her parents, especially the beatings. She did send a wire to them informing them of his death and she would be back home after his affairs were handled. She did say she was staying with Aunt Margaret which was more to ease her mother's mind than hers. She asked the sheriff to send a wire to Lucas' father explaining him of his son's death and that he would be buried here unless he wanted other arrangements made.

A wire came back the next day short and sweet. *Dear Sheriff Wilson, thank you for your wire informing me of my son's passing. On the arrangements you've stated on the resting place of his remains it makes no difference to me. His mother and I felt we lost our son some time ago. Sincerely Judge Andrew Walsh.* It seemed no one wanted Lucas. It was almost a pity no one felt for him. In due time, Colleen gave birth to a baby girl who she named Margret Colleen Walsh. Margaret who became a second mother to the girl after the death of her husband was thrilled with her choice of the name.

~~~~~~~

In the winter of 1898, the harsh weather almost wiped out many of the herds in Colorado. Both Lucky Shamrock and Autumn Sky had lost a considerable amount of stock. Yet they managed to hold on to what was left. If it was one thing Tom taught them all, if one
~~~~~~~

was to survive, one must never give up. One must fight for everything that is worthwhile in life. It was just about dusk when the snow started up again with the strong winds, it was hard to see anything out the windows. But Katherine managed to see what she thought were two strangers walking in the snow. She called Trace to the window, "Trace, I think there are two people out there, we have to get the inside."

Trace looks out the window and though the dusk was getting darker and the wind was picking up, there was definitely two people trying to walk through the snow drifts. He grabs his coat and heads for the door, followed by Shayleen and Katherine. He looks at Shayleen, "you stay here." She was about to protest when he stated, "I don't know who these folks are and if it isn't someone I want in the house, I don't want to worry about you being out there too. Autumn, just stay here by the door." She looks at him, "but..."

He looks at her with that stare and silenced her. He opens the door and slowly makes his way down the steps and on to the mounds of snow where a path once was.

Katherine went back to the window and watched as Trace slowly made his way to the two strangers. From the door, Shayleen watched Trace reach them and appeared to be talking to them, then all three were heading for the house. Reaching the door, Trace smiled at Shayleen, "I have a surprise for you Autumn."

She steps back to let the others in. As they take off their coats, Trace smiles at his wife, "look who was out there wandering in this blizzard."

As the stranger takes off his coat, he smiles at her, "hi Irish."

She is totally shocked, "Buck? Oh my, is it really you?" She runs into his arms. "Buck Matthews, why I never thought I would ever see you again."

"Well, I didn't think I'd be back here, also, but well…" He turned and helped the other stranger remove the coat and revealed the stranger was a woman, a very pregnant woman. "Irish, Trace, this is Lunata, my wife."

"Your wife, why Buck, that's wonderful news."

He looked at his wife, "Lunata, these are my dear friends, this is Irish, Trace and that beautiful lady standing by the fire is Katherine." He walks over to her and gives her a hug, "I remembered you told me to come back."

"I did, and I'm so glad you did."

Shayleen looks at him, "so tell us Buck, are you here to stay or just passing through?"

He looks at them, "well I was hoping to get a job and..." before he could finish, Shayleen and Trace both said together, "you're hired."

He smiled at them, "thanks."

"Hey it's us who should thank you, you were always one of our best hands. Heck, with you and Chance, you two helped Papa get this place where it is."

He looks around, "by the way, where is Tom, I'd love to see him."

A silence came over the room, then Shayleen spoke, "we lost him ten years ago Buck."

Buck bowed his head; he had not known. Tom was good to him and gave him the means to be just like any other human being. Never treating him like a ranch hand, he was more like family. Yes, Tom was a man among men. He looks at Irish," I'm sorry Irish, I didn't know."

She gives him a hug, "I know Buck, but I think he's happy you're here with us now."

Katherine who had gone into the kitchen comes back with some hot coffee and she had managed to find something for Buck and Lunata to eat. As she hands a plate to Buck and to Lunata, "I hope you two are a bit hungry."

Buck smiled at her, "Katherine, you know I wouldn't say no to your cooking."

As the evening moved on Buck, Trace, Shayleen and even Katherine renewed old ties in the same room they now were in. So, any memories that tied them all to the family. In a sense, Buck was always family and now he was home again. It was just before midnight when Buck decided he and Lunata would head off to the barn to make arrangements for their sleeping quarters.

It was Shayleen who stood up and refused to hear of such an idea. "You are staying right here Buck, bedroom upstairs and we don't expect the children home for another three days. Now you and your wife head on upstairs and pick out a nice soft bed and get a good night's rest."

Chapter 5

With everyone finally settled in their rooms, Shayleen is sitting on the bed as Trace walks over and places another log on the fire and then walks over to the bed taking off his shirt. She looks at him, "is it still snowing out there?"

Trace nods, "yes, still coming down. "Buck and Lunata were lucky they got this far. They should have turned back after the first start of the storm. Buck knows the signs of a blizzard." He slowly gets into bed and Shayleen snuggles up to him.

"Well, they probably thought they could keep each other warm. There are many ways to do that you know." She gently kisses his cheek, "I can think of many to get warm." She moves closer to him and he looks into her eyes," so could I Mrs. Cooper, so could I."

He begins to leave a trail of kisses down her neck as she gently unties her night gown and he takes it off and lies it on the bed. His touch sent flames of passion in her that could melt any blizzard. Her hands roamed freely on his chest as they moved downward. His passions mounted as he looked into her eyes. He was lost in the depth and passion of this woman who owned his heart and soul. They rose to their passions again and again and when exhausted they lay in each other's arms totally content to remain there for the rest of their lives.

It was just before daybreak when Shayleen heard a knock on the door. It was Katherine calling, "Shayleen? Are you up?" Slowly she sat up and placed her night gown back on and walked quietly to the door and opened it. "Is there something wrong?"

Katherine looked at her, "it's Lunata, I think it's time for her baby. I'm going to need your help."

She nodded, "let me get dressed and I'll get Trace up."

Katherine closed the door and Shayleen hurried to get dressed, then went over to Trace still sleeping, "Trace get up, I need your help!"

He opens one eye and looks up at his wife. "what's wrong, is it morning already?"

She gets on the bed and takes his face in her hands, "Trace Cooper, I need you to open your eyes now! I need you to be with Buck, Lunata is having the baby."

He opens his eyes and looks at her. He jumps up from the bed and starts looking for his pants. He was completely awake at this point and ready to follow her next order. "I'm ready Autumn."

She looks at him and smiles, "I'm glad you're ready, but I think you should be dressed with a bit more than what you have on now."

He looked down and saw he only had his thermals on and his boots. He stumbles to get his boots off as

Shayleen grabs her shoes and heads out the door to the room down the hall. As Shayleen opened the door to rush inside, she was met head on with Buck who was heading downstairs to boil water for Katherine. Though one always wondered why the request for boiling water was needed it was still a way to keep fathers away from the room and it did work. The two men kept a vigil at the foot of the stairs to notice any movement from the room, yet nothing was happening. The hours dragged on and no sounds came from that room.

Suddenly, Shaylen appears at the top of the stairs holding a bundle in her arms. She smiles down at Buck, "Buck, would you like to come up and meet your daughter?"

He didn't have to be told twice. He started up those stairs taking the steps two and three at a time. When he finally reached the top, Shayleen pulled back the blanket and Buck got to see his daughter. "She's beautiful Irish."

"That she is Buck, I can't deny that."

He looks at her, "Lunata?"

Shayleen smiles, "she's fine you can go in and see her in a while."

Trace walks up the stairs and behind Buck to get a glimpse of the baby, "she's beautiful Buck."

Buck looks over and smiles at him. Shayleen once again puts the blanket over her and starts to head for the room. "I believe this little lady has had enough excitement for now. With that she opens the bedroom door and disappears. A few moments later she appears this time to tell Buck he can go in and see his wife.

Trace takes her hand and they head down the stairs and get ready for a new day. Outside the snow had stopped, but it left quite a bit of it all over. Trace looks out the back door, "looks like it's going to take a while before I can get to the barn to milk the cow."

It wasn't too long after that, Shayleen was busy trying to get breakfast started when Katherine came down with the baby in her arms. "Katherine what are you doing with the baby?"

She gently sits down on the nearby chair and smiles down at the baby, "oh I just thought I'd give Buck and Lunata some time to themselves."

Trace walks over to her and sits down. "Seems having time to themselves is what caused this little one." He smiles down and takes her hand in his. He looks at Shayleen, "Hey Autumn, do you ever think about..."

She stopped him before he could finish, "I think I'll settle for grandchildren at this point in my life."

As they are enjoying the baby, Buck happened to walk in the kitchen with Lunata. It was Katherine who noticed her, "Lunata, what are you doing up?"

"Oh, please Miss Katherine, I have stayed too long in bed I must help..."

Shayleen looked up at her, "Lunata, don't be silly, you're a guest here and after all, you just had this beautiful little girl."

Buck stepped in, "Ah yes, about our little girl, we talked about it and Lunata and I agree we'd like to name her Irish Katherine Mathews after you two ladies of course."

Katherine looked at them, "why Buck, I am deeply honored as I know Shayleen is also."

Shayleen gets up and hugs Buck, "you have made me very proud, my brother and I will always be the little sister you watched over."

The following day the snow started to melt though one couldn't see the ground yet the fir trees started to show their green through patches of snow still on the branches weighing them down. It was in the kitchen that Shayleen was trying to get breakfast started. She walks over to the stove when Trace walks in and right into her and the bowl of fresh eggs she's holding, sending them to the floor. "Trace Cooper!!"

"I'm sorry Autumn, I guess I wasn't looking, I..."

She looked at the mess on the floor and was almost ready to cry, "That was breakfast, now what am I going to do?"

He looks at her and smiles, "don't worry, I'll get you some more, you just start the bacon and I'll be right back." He heads toward the back door and once outside

Shayleen here's a thump. She rushes to the door to see Trace sitting in a pile of snow. "Trace!"

He tries to get up and falls back down again, sending both of them into laughter. She helps him back up and together they fall. This went on for another time until Buck entered the kitchen smelling the bacon burning in the frying pan and looking for them. He looks out the door and smile, "when you two get finished out there, you might want to check on the bacon, it's extra crispy in here."

Breakfast was eventually made, but it was nothing to do with bacon or eggs, it was bread and jam with coffee. Not the heartiest meal, but then again, there was no other choice his morning. As they sat down to the bread and jam, Trace looked at his wife, "seems we're not very good in the kitchen, perhaps we should stick to the bedroom, we don't seem to have any problems in there."

Buck almost gags on the coffee with that remark and Shayleen looks at her husband, "Trace Cooper, I'll thank you to keep a civil tongue in your mouth after all, we have guests."

Trace looks at Buck, "you mean Buck, heck Honey, he's family, he knows us and..."

"Trace!!!!!"

~~~~~~

Two weeks had passed and since Buck and Lunata's baby was born. Both mother and daughter were getting
~~~~~~

stronger each day. With the roads able to pass again Shayleen and Trace thought it a good time to head in to town for supplies especially since the children would be coming in in two weeks for the holidays. Leaving Buck home with the ladies, Shayleen and Trace head for town. As they got closer to the general store, they noticed a large group had gathered near the sheriff's office. Trace looks at Shayleen. "what's going on there?" As they closer they hear the voice of Joshua Blackthorne.

~~~~~~

Seems the snow had forced the wolves down from the mountains and they were attacking Blackthorne's cattle. He looks over at Trace and Shayleen as they get off the wagon. Even though years had passed, Josh never did forget or forgive the woman who told him off in church in front of the whole congregation.

Shayleen smiles at the men that had gathered and then makes her way into the store.

Billy Cummings stops Trace as he follows his wife. "Trace, can I have a word with you?"

Shayleen looks at him, "go ahead, I'll get the supplies."

They both nod to her and she goes in the store.

"Trace, I want to ask you, do you have any trouble with wolves attacking your cattle? The reason I'm asking is Blackthorne says his cows are attacked every night, says he's losing four to five head each night, due to the
~~~~~~

wolves. He's asking for men to form groups and guard the herds each night."

Trace leans against the door and looks at the boy, "Billy, I know you've seen the snow fall we had last weekend and the week before that, also, and it's safe to assume that the wildlife has suffered due to the weather and we, also, know that these critters are just looking for food. for them to take four to five cows a night is a bit of stretching the truth don't you think? Look, if it's a few cows that get lost, I'll be happy to supply a herd of five to keep everyone happy 'cause I do know it's not four or five a night. Look, you know as well as I do you send these men up in the mountains with a gun and they'll end up shooting themselves or worse. "

"I know Trace, but I do think these wolves are getting close to town."

"Billy, wolves are loners, and they ain't getting close to town, they ain't stupid, matter of fact, if the humans thought like they did, it would sure be an easier world out here."

The boy looks at him, "but Mr. Blackthorne said..."

"Billy, you know he's quick to shoot anything that's a threat to him, even after all these years, he hasn't learned."

Billy nods his head and walks back to the group of men, and Trace joins his wife.

Shayleen has just finished the shopping and smiles at Trace. "Well, you're just in time to pay the bill."

He looks at Tim, "how much did she spend this time?"

Shayleen looked at both of them, "now gentlemen, I only bought the necessities."

Trace looks at the two boxes on the counter and the two packages in her hands, "Oh I'm sure of that."

Tim follows them out carrying one of the boxes. As Trace helps his wife on the wagon, Shayleen looks at Tim, "now don't forget Tim, I'll be back in a week when the children arrive. I want you and your family to join us for supper that night."

He smiles up at her, "we'll be there Ma'am, thank you for the invite."

She looks across the street and sees Blackthorne looking at her. Trace gets on the wagon and she looks at him, "what's that old wind bag stirring up now?"

"Wolves."

"Wolves?"

"Near as I hear the story is the wolves are coming down from the mountains looking for food and seem to like Blackthorne cattle, seems they take four to five a night."

She looks at him, "mighty hungry and strong wolves taking that many a night."

"Seems that no other steers interest them"

She looks at him as they ride out of town, "Damn a shame up until now, I thought they had better taste, than to pick on his stock.'"

Trace just shook his head and drove on.

~~~~~~

A week passed and with the weather warming up, the wolves attacking began to die down. It seemed the roads were clear enough that the stages and even the trains were once again able to pass through. It was a relief for Shayleen to get the wire from Mick stating he and the others would be arriving on Friday afternoon. It was the moment Shayleen has been waiting for. To have the whole family together.

Trace walks into the kitchen and sees Katherine at the stove. "Katherine, it's so good to see you there. We know what happens when Autumn is by the stove.'

Katherine looks at him, "now Trace, that's not fair. I have seen her by the stove many times and nothing has happened. It's only when the two of you are in the room together, things happen. Come to think of it when you two are in any room..." she stops when there is a knock on the door.

Trace answers the door to find Billy Cummings standing there. "Billy, come on in, would you like a cup of coffee?" He looks the boy. "Is there something wrong Billy?"
~~~~~~

"Well see, there's been a few ranchers and there seems to be a problem with their cattle being killed."

"Wolves again?"

"No sir, it appears to be a big cat."

Trace looks at the boy, "You saying we've got a mountain lion out there and he's hungry?"

"That's what Jim Murdoch said, by the time he got to his prize bull, the poor thing was torn to pieces."

Trace looks at the boy, "have any of the other ranchers had any problems?"

Shayleen walks in as she only hears the last comment and decides to add her opinion, "well, is Mr. Blackthorne deciding to form another hunting party to track down this creature also. I mean he'll soon have the entire country-side hunting this poor creature and every ranchers ranch will be left on its own."

Billy looks at her, "I know Mrs. Cooper and that's why I am worried."

She looks at them both, "well, Trace is not helping to have this animal destroyed nor are any of our hands."

Trace looks at her, "Irish, this cat is eating cattle and..."

"That animal is only looking for food, I will not allow anyone on this ranch to kill it." She looks at them with determination. It's a look they have seen in her face many times before and a look not to be reckoned with. She turns and walks into the kitchen.

Trace looks at Billy, "I'll go check on the herds later and if I find or see anything, I'll come in and let you know."

"Thanks Trace. Say I'm sorry I got Mz. Cooper all upset..."

"'Don't worry about Autumn Son, she'll get over it."

As Billy leaves, Buck comes down the stairs. "Trouble?"

"Not really, seems a mountain lion has come down from the high country and he's taking a few cows. Billy was just asking for me to check our herd."

"If you like, I'll be happy to go up there with you to check things out."

"Thanks, I think we can get some breakfast first, besides Katherine's cooking now."

It was a quiet breakfast as Shayleen refused to talk about the reason for Billy's visit. When Trace and Buck left, Buck was the only one who looked back to see only Lunata on the porch to see them ride off, Shayleen didn't even say goodbye. Buck looked at Trace, "seems Irish is still mad, I've never seen her not say goodbye."

"Oh she's still mad and will probably be mad when we get back, but she'll be her old self again when the kids get here in a few days.

They had only gone five miles when they ran into Blackthorne and his men. They were hunting for the cat.

Blackthorne looked at Trace, "It's not too safe out here with that cat loose Cooper."

"Seems ya'll ain't worried, but then again, with all these guns around you, why would you be? Tell me, do you really need an army to go out and catch one cat?"

Blackthorne smiles, "oh there will be more than this, I've posted a thousand-dollar bounty for the man who kills that cat and brings it back to town."

Buck looks at him, "sure do hope your men look first and make sure what they hit."

Blackthorne who still after all these years had no love for Indians looks at him, "don't you go worrying about that Injun, we all know what we are shooting at." Blackthorne never did forget that Buck survived that day his men raided Buck's ranch and killed his wife.

Buck still remembers the faces of those men as they shot him and left him for dead. Suddenly, shots rang out and Blackthorne and his men race across the ridge.

"Think they got him Trace?"

"Not a chance, that cat's too smart for Blackthorne."

Chapter 6

Evening was setting in and still Trace and Buck had not returned. Lunata was sitting by the fire rocking the baby as Shayleen looked out the window looking for them to return. *'At least they should have the good sense to come home before it got dark'* she thought. As the sun disappears behind the mountain, she begins to worry. Suddenly, the door opens and Buck walks in followed by Trace. Shayleen runs to her husband and jumps into his arms as he lifts her in the air and kisses her. "Maybe I should come home like this more often."

Buck smiles as he walks over to his wife and gently places a kiss on her forehead.

Shayleen looks at Trace, "it was beginning to get dark and I was starting to worry..."

"I knew you would be, but I'm here right now, so you can stop worrying." He leans down and kisses her again.

As they ate supper, Trace was happy to report there were signs that the cat had gotten off their herd. As the night wore on, each one went off to bed leaving Trace and Shayleen by the fire. He took his wife in his arms and drew her closer to him. "I hope they never find him." There was no need to tell Trace what she was thinking. He knew her mind was on that cat. "You seem to have a bond with that animal."

"I just find it a bit silly to go all over the countryside for one cat. Is losing a few head of cows mean that much?"

"You know Thunder Sky would say you have a bond with this animal." She looks up and smiles at him as he smiles at her, "you and those cat eyes of yours."

"Trace, do you ever miss the old days?"

He looks down at her, "sometimes. But I have all my days with you and that makes life happier."

She gazed into the fire and thought about Thunder Sky. The gentle man who treated her like his own daughter.

Trace turned and looked at her, "he loved you too." After all these years Trace always seemed to know where her thoughts were.

~~~~~~

The following morning, everyone was up early. Shayleen and Trace were preparing to head into town to meet the children coming in on the train, fifteen miles from town, Tad Cooper is looking out the train car window, "look Pop, we're getting close to home."

Mike smiles and continues talking to his brother-in - aw Sam. "Seems Tad is excited to get back home." Mick smiles, "I guess three weeks in Deaver was 'enough for the boy. I thought he would enjoy it more."

"Well, you know that boy is a born rancher."
~~~~~~

Across from them, Katherine is sitting with her children and Colleen's little one year old Maria is across with her son, Mick and daughter Shay. Colleen and Margaret Cummings are up closer to the front of the car. "Mama's gonna be so surprised to see you." Margaret smiles.

"I know. Tim doesn't even know I'm coming, I had wished Tim could have joined us, but he'll take the next one on Friday, at least we'll all be here for the holiday."

The train was coming along the side of the mountain when the sound of gun fire was heard. Not by those in the train, but those on the other side of the mountain trying to get the cat. As the passengers continue to chat, outside no one seems to notice the snow on the side of the mountain starting to move slowly down the side. Suddenly, there is a rumbling and snow, ice, rocks and trees began to fall down the mountain with such force, it destroyed everything in its path. The train tried to avoid the debris as it plundered into the cars sending three of them off the tracks and plunging into the icy grave below. Within minutes, the remaining three cars and the engine were hanging on the tracks by the grace of God. Inside the cars was total darkness, except for a few streams of light that streamed in from the broken windows. The windows of the cars were completely broken from the snow and tree trunks that plummeted in with the fall. Mick managed to move and finally stand up and try to move.

The debris was blocking all sides of him, yet he had to look for Maria and the children. "Maria! Maria! "He turns as he hears a muffled sound. "Maria? It's me Pop. "

"What happened?"

"Tad, are you all alright?"

Again, the boy answers, "I guess so, I can't see anyone can you see anybody Pop?"

Suddenly Sam's voice is heard, "Mick, I'm here with Katherine and the children, we do have quite a few folks that are hurt pretty bad."

Mick realizes they are trapped here with no one out there knowing they are there or alive.

~~~~~~

On the other side of the mountain, the sounds of cheers were heard. Joshua Blackthorne had killed the cat. It took him four shots, but he did kill the animal. As he stood there looking at the dead animal, he felt rather proud of himself that he took down the animal himself and two, he didn't have to pay anyone that bounty. As he stood there, he felt he once again had conquered an enemy. What he didn't realize, his little hunting expedition and the sound of the successive gun shots that had loosened the snow, causing the avalanche and the derailing and quite possibly the deaths of many on that train. Of course, that never entered his mind.
~~~~~~

Mick makes his way toward his wife climbing over piles of snow and rock and reaches them. He puts his arms around Maria and thanks the Lord she's safe. "Mick what happened?"

"Avalanche, near as I can figure. But for the life of me I have no idea what triggered it off."

"Sam, Sam, where are you?"

Slowly, the car tilted and the entire windows on the left side went crashing to the bottom of the mountain. With that came sunlight and the other fear. The train was indeed resting on the tracks with only one side still on the tracks. Any movement and the entire train engine and all would end in the bottom on the mountain.

Sam looks down from the whole in the side of the engine, then looks back at Mick, "well, is this where we wonder about that so called Irish luck, I've heard about all these years?"

Paul Carlson was on the north range of his property when his younger son, Joey, spotted the train, "Pa, look at the train!" Paul looks up and sees the train truly is in trouble. "Joey, you get on that horse of yours and ride into town and get the sheriff.'"

In town waiting on the platform for the train was Trace and Shayleen. They didn't notice Tim walking up to them. "Well, I see you're waiting for the train from Denver."

"Well, you know Autumn, she insisted on being here early."

Suddenly from the outskirts of town they see Joey Paulson riding up fast. "Tim! Tim! There's been an accident, the train..." The boy jumped off his horse and ran up to Tim, "Sheriff Tim, Pa says to come quick, train wreck bad..."

Grace gently puts his hands on the boy's shoulder, "Joey, where is the train wreck and are there any passengers?"

The boy looks at him, "I don't know Mr. Cooper, Pa told me to come into town."

Tim went over to the outside of the general store and took out his gun and fired four shots in the air. The signal that there was trouble. Townsfolk were coming out from all over. Tim looked at them, "Joey here has just come in to tell me there was a train wreck outside of town. Now I'm gonna need wagons, blankets, ropes, and anything else to help these folks. Let's start out as soon as we can."

With that, the people began to scatter to get the supplies. Trace looks at Tim, if it's all right with you, we'll head off now."

At the sight, Paul Carlson's men had already started to shore up the cars to level them on the tracks. Three of his men had climbed on the tops of the cars opening the tops, letting not only the sunlight in, but water and bandages.

The sound of the digging gave those inside peace of mind that someone was out there and they would get out. From inside the main car, Mick began to search for his sister Colleen. "She was sitting there with Mick, her and Aunt Margaret, oh Mick you don't think..."

Mick lifts the seat and sees Colleen. Gently he lifts her from the pile of wreckage. Her body covered in blood a gaping wound at her side and her eyes wide open, but seeing nothing. The sight of her sister's body sent sobs from Katherine's throat. Poor Colleen had suffered to with her husband, now with her plans to come back home and start a new life with her daughter, now that was gone. Mick gently places his sister down and Sam covers her with his jacket.

Katherine looks at them, "what about Aunt Katherine? She was sitting with Colleen."

Mick looks at her, "Katie, I promise I'll look for Aunt Margaret as soon as we move this rubbish."

Sam slowly takes out another body. An elderly man, barely alive, yet still breathing. Mick helps Sam lay the man down and starts back. Suddenly, Trace's voice is heard from above. "Mick, Son, how is the situation down there."

"Pa!"

"I'm here Mick, now how many are injured.?"

"We have a lot with cuts and broken bones in this car. I counted so far four dead counting Aunt Margaret and Katherine."

Trace bows his head for a moment, he realizes one of his daughters is gone. It took a few moments, then Trace regains his composure. "Okay Mick, we're gonna start taking the bodies down, the children first, I'll let you know when we're ready. It took a few tries, but Trace managed to get a crew to help get the children out first safely, then the injured. Gently, the men tied the body of Colleen to the make-shift stretcher and eased her down the side of the car. It was a very determined man who watched the body of her daughter slowly being lowered from the train.

Once she had seen both Colleen and Margaret, she quietly moved to the wagon and sat in silence. She sat in the wagon dealing with her grief. Trying to accept the fact that on that last wagon, there lay the body of her daughter. She closed her eyes and started to pray. As she began to remember the words, she heard the voice of her father. "Shayla, can ye hear me Lass?" She opened her eyes, "Popa?"

"You are a strong one my Lass, you need not grieve, the young one is here with me and your mother. Dry your eyes Lassie, it was her time to come home. You have to watch over her little one."

"But why Papa, she was so young."

"Take care of those living Lassie, they need you. Take care of her little one, you have to teach her so much."

Suddenly, his voice was gone and Trace was standing near the wagon. He looked up at her, "everything okay?"

"Trace I heard Papa. Just as clear as I hear you." She looked at him, "you don't believe me."

He looked at her, "oh I believe you Autumn, I believe anything you tell me."

She looked at him, "Trace, he wants us to raise Colleen's little girl."

Trace looks at her, "that's no problem."

"But Trace, you can't mean..."

"Autumn Sky, you can and will raise that child."

Chapter 7

The following morning, Matt Cooper heard about the train wreck and rode from Manitou straight to Colorado Springs, since the trains were not running due to the wreck. Shayleen sits by the fire as Trace walks to the door to answer the knock. He opens the door and sees Matthew, the look on his father's face tells him tragedy has hit the family. "I got here as soon as I could Pa."

"Your mother is in the living room."

Slowly, Matt walks into the room and sees his mother sitting the fire dressed in black. She looks up as he makes his way toward her. The sight of her youngest son eased some of the pain she was feeling. He looked at her. "Momma?"

"Matt I'm glad you're here."

"Momma."

"I am so glad you're here and safe."

Suddenly, little Maggie walks over to her Uncle Matt and tugs at his coat. He stoops down and takes his little niece in his arms, "Hi Katic, how's my big girl?"

She gives him a hug and sees Katherine walk into the room. "Matt!"

He walks over to her, "hello Grandma!" He gives her a hug, "I'm so glad our here and safe."

Shayleen gets up and walks toward the window, she knows they would have to get ready to head for town Colleen's funeral was today. She looked at the window asking why? Why did she have to die? It wasn't right for a parent to bury their child, but she promised Trace she would be strong for all of them. She turns when she hears Chance's voice He smiled at her, "morning Irish. Charity and I decided to ride into town with you all, if that's alright."

Chance turns and sees Matt walk in the door. "Matt, I'm glad to see you Son." Chance shakes Matt's hand and pats his shoulder.

"I'm glad to be here too," Chance looks at the boy who was like a son to him and was only two years older than his own son Andrew. It was at that moment Charity walked in to see Shayleen. She sees Matt and greets him, "Matthew!"

Matt looks at her, "Aunt Charity, good to see you."

After the welcomes the room became somber again. It was true everyone knew what was to take place today, yet the sorrow could not continue until it destroyed them.

It was Matt who unlike the others had no idea of how the accident happened and felt to ignore what happened was not the answer to move on from this tragedy.

Chance was the first to offer his opinion, "some say with the snow starting to become too heavy on the top of the mountains, the weight started to make the ground underneath shift and for whatever reason, it caused the avalanche."

Back in town, Blackthorn's men were celebrating that they or should one say, Blackthorne killed the cat that was raiding the ranchers' cows.

Judy Lynn Cummings was in the general store when she heard two of the ranchers boast on how Blackthorne killed the cat himself after only firing three shots. She walks over to where they were standing and began talking to them. "Forgive me Gentlemen, I couldn't help but overhear your conversation, you say Mr. Blackthorne killed the lion himself?"

The cowhand smiled at her, "Yes ma'am, we was all there and Mr. Blackthorne saw that cat just as bold as brass standing on that ledge just a lookin' at him."

Judy looked at the cowhand, "oh my, that would surely have terrified me."

The ranch hand smiled at her and continued his story, "maybe so Ma'am, but not ole' Josh, why he set his sights on that cat three times in a row. The cat fell in his tracks."

She looked at the other cowhand who was nodding yes to the account of the story. "Well, all I can say Gentlemen is that we all here in town are grateful for Mr. Blackthorne." She was about to leave, when she turned to the cowhands again, "you said he shot the cat on the south ridge?"

"Yes Ma'am it was the south ridge."

"And there were no other men shooting?"

"No Ma'am, just Mr. Blackthorne."

"Well like I said, the town and people have a lot to thank him for." As Judy heads out of the store, Billy walks in. He smiles at his sister-in-law who quietly takes him aside away from the others. "Billy I just heard Blackthorne killed the mountain lion yesterday."

"Good, maybe this bounty huntin' thing will be done with."

"Billy, you're not listening, they were on the south ridge when thy killed the cat."

He looked at his sister-in-law and knew what she was thinking, but before he did anything, he had to be sure. He walked over to the ranch hands, "howdy boys, you say you shot the cat on the south ridge?"

"Yes sir Deputy, Mr. Blackthorne got him with three shots."

"Well I was wondering if you boys would like to show me where it happened?"

The shorter one looked at him wondering why Billy was so interested in where the cat was killed, but still was happy to show him. "Sure Deputy, but there ain't nothing there now."

They walk out of the store and Judy watches them get on their horses and ride out of town. Judy looks up at the clock and realizes it's almost time for Collen's service.

~~~~~~

Across town the church was beginning to fill with townspeople to say goodbye to one of the Cooper children and to Margaret Cummings. Everyone knew Colleen Cooper; she had grown up here with her grandfather was one of the founding citizens of the town. Margaret Cummings another fine woman, her husband and her also had their roots deep in this town. Both women liked by all and greatly missed by their loved ones and the town are laid to rest today. Siting in the
~~~~~~

front row were: Shayleen, Trace, Buck. Charity Katherine, Buck and Lunata. Behind them, Katherine, Sam, Mick, Maria, and Matt. The children and grandchildren were in the following seats. Shayleen held on to Trace's hand through the whole ceremony never letting go of it once. He was the rock and together they would hold the family together.

~~~~~~

She looked at him, who had told her he had nothing to give her, but his heart and soul and would love her all his days had given her so much. Trace looks at her, his Autumn Sky, so brave and strong. She was his strength; her spirit would be bound to his all their days and beyond. He was rich in ways only others can dream of. She gave him all he ever wanted in life and her love for him would never die.

On the south ridge, Billy and the cowhands came to the spot where Blackthorne killed the cat. "Right here Deputy, here is where Mr. Blackthorne killed the cat." Billy got off his horse and looked around. He saw everything looked normal until he walked over to the other side. Looking down, he saw a sight that filled him with anger and rage. There below was the twisted wreckage of the train. Anger began to build inside of him. He called to the cow hands, "you two come over here."

"What's wrong Deputy?"
~~~~~~

He points to the bottom, "you two take a good look at that."

The shorter one looks at him, "We don't know nothing 'bout that Deputy."

"You two hear me and hear me good, you go home and tell that boss of yours, I want to see him in my office today or I'll be out to get him."

"Deputy we..."

"Get out of here now!" They mounted their horses and rode off.

Billy realizes he's missed his mother's service, yet he found what caused not only her death, but the others as well.

Chapter 8

Blackthorne's men delivered the deputy's message to their boss, but Blackthorne sent another hand to tell the deputy he would be in the following morning, he had pressing issues at the ranch he needed to do.

That evening ole' Josh sat by the fire with a bottle of whisky in his hand as he went over in his head the shooting. He had no idea that the shots he fired did set off the avalanche or not. The more he thought of it the more he was sure he had to go and look for himself. Since it was late, he decided not to bother the ranch hands, besides he knew the land as good, if not better than them. He mounted his horse and not able to steady himself in the saddle, he held on to the reins with one hand and the bottle in the other as he rode off into the night. Stumbling off his horse he wanders to the spot where he shot the cat. He takes a swig from the bottle, but its empty and he throws it across the snow. "Can't see a fool thing out here." Suddenly, he hears the roar of a cat. He mumbles to himself, "now Josh, you know you got that cat two days ago. Ain't nothing out here, it could be just the wind playing tricks on you." The sound came again. As he turned, from nowhere a cat leaped on him. His screams went unheard in the night. Alone on the mountain, Joshua Blackthorne fought his last demon. It was as if justice had been served on that mountain with the ending of Joshua Blackthorne.

The next morning Billy Cummings was summoned to the ranch by the foreman. They had been searching since day light for their boss and found his body on the south ridge. Billy walked over to the body and lifted the blanket, it was not a pretty sight. There wasn't much left of his body, the cat had torn him apart pretty good.

"Can anyone tell me why did he go out on his own?"

"We didn't even hear him ride out Deputy."

"Did you see any other tracks, I mean of another cat?"

The hands all shook their heads no. "That's just it, there were no tracks, but Mr. Blackthorne's and the horse. Matter of fact, it was the horse coming back to the ranch that told us something was wrong."

He looks at the men, "well, you can get him to the undertakers and make the arrangements. I'll take a look up on the ridge and head back into town. Meanwhile, don't go looking for any cats or anything else up there."

The first ranch Billy hit was the Lucky Shamrock. He thought about holding off, after all they had been through, but he had job to do. He was greeted by Katherine, "morning Billy, won't you come in."

"Mz. Katherine, is Trace around?"

"Yes we're all in the kitchen, will you join us."

He follows Katherine into the kitchen, "Sit down Billy, can I get you a cup of coffee?"

"No, no thank you Ma'am."

Shayleen smiles at him, "how's your mom?"

"She's fine Ma'am."

Shayleen sees Billy is a bit uncomfortable, "Trace, why don't you and Billy go to the study and talk."

They leave the kitchen and walk across into the study where Billy tells him about his theory on the avalanche.

Trace looks at him, "you mean Blackthorne's shots caused the death of all those people and my daughter?"

"Looks that way Trace."

"Where is he, I want him hung, no, I want to kill him with my bare hands!"

Billy looks at him. "he's dead."

"Dead?"

"Seems old Blackthorne went up to the south ridge to see for himself if his shots really did cause the avalanche. Near as I can figure it, he was up there alone and drunk and well seems like the cat didn't take too kindly him killing the other and well it wasn't pretty sight."

Trace looked at Billy, it wasn't a cat Billy. It wasn't."

"But Trace, I saw the body or what was left of it."

"Blackthorne finally met his last demon and ghosts is what killed him. It's like a story my father told me, seems there was this young brave and he was away from his camp hunting for food. When he came back, his family were killed by white men. The brave asked the Great

Spirit to let him live so he could find those who did this and kill them. The brave roamed for years looking for these men. Some say he never died. Others say he takes on the form of animals avenging the death of others, my best advice to you Billy, is let it go. Let the dead bury the dead. Save and protect the living."

"You might be right Trace, but I still need to tell the others to stay close to home just till we're sure it really wasn't a cat."

They head to leave, when Shayleen is standing on the other side of the door, ready to knock. "Oh you're leaving, I was just about to join you."

Trace puts his arm around her shoulder as they escort Billy to the door, "well thanks for the advice, Billy and I'll look into that this afternoon."

Shayleen looked at them knowing they were not about to let her know what they were talking about. "Are you two planning something?"

"Bye Billy."

Trace leans down and kisses his wife cheek, "I'll tell you later when we're upstairs."

THE END

Reviews of Cheyenne Autumn Sky

Set back in the 1800's makes a really good read.If you like romance, you'll love this three part series with Shayleen and the others. A true love story at it's best. Book review café.

The book will have you feeling excited, cheerful and upbeat. The book is fanciful, entertaining, emotional and playful. The ending wraps up everything. Western magazine

Very good book Historical Regency Review

Come to the world of Shayleen O'Malley and see if you can figure out who her true love is this one may surprise you I enjoy books with happy ending and this one fits the bill.Shirley Johnson reviewer

Praise for the Autumn Sky series by Shirley Johnson

I was captured upon reading of the author's first installment relating to the life of Shayleen, a spunky young woman. Shayleen, after having drawn the hearts of two wonderful men discovered where her choice has taken her. Living in the 1800s, we find in this second book, Shayleen has married the mountain man Trace.

I smiled as I read of the joyous life she's living, loved by a wonderful man, blessed with several children surrounded by close friends and family, she had everything any woman could ask for, until her world was shattered and her life would change forever. He removes the general Custer and all of his men were massacred sent the territory into a time of deep hate between Indian and the white man. The author takes you into the soul of Shayleen as she struggles with the injustices that are running rampant in the land she loves. We travel with her through them, through her life, bear with her the loss of friends and family, times and places. We rejoice with her over the birth of more children and the victory she receives in her battle against those who breed hatred toward the natives of the land.

The author brings to life all that has happened to the characters that we have come to know and love from the first book weaving them into the storyline and bringing them into the heart of their existence. There are so many happenings in this book some joyous, some heartbreak.

This book is about life, death, fear, hope and eternity.